The Magic Nesting Doll

Jacqueline K. Ogburn

Illustrated by Laurel Long

Dial Books

Published by Dial Books
A division of Penguin Putnam Inc.
345 Hudson Street
New York, New York 10014

Text copyright © 2000 by Jacqueline K. Ogburn
Illustrations copyright © 2000 by Laurel Long
All rights reserved
Designed by Nancy R. Leo-Kelly
Text set in Cochin
Printed in Hong Kong on acid-free paper
1 3 5 7 9 10 8 6 4 2

Library of Congress Cataloging-in-Publication Data
Ogburn, Jacqueline K.
The magic nesting doll/by Jacqueline K. Ogburn; illustrated by Laurel Long.—1st ed.
p.   cm.
Summary: After her grandmother dies, Katya finds herself in a kingdom where
the Tsarevitch has been turned into living ice, and she uses the magic nesting dolls her
grandmother had given her to try to break the curse.
ISBN 0-8037-2414-4
[1. Fairy tales.] I. Long, Laurel, ill. II. Title.
PZ8.03Mag 2000   [E]—dc21   98-34397   CIP   AC

The art for this book was created using oil paints on watercolor paper primed with gesso.

❧ *Author's Note* ❧

The matryoshka, or Russian nesting doll, was developed in the 1890's by a group of fine artists and craftsmen interested in Russian folk art, known as the Mamontov Circle. A combination of the traditional crafts of nested wooden objects and fine enamel painting, the first matryoshka was designed by artist S.V. Malyutin and crafted by master toy-maker V. Zvezdochkin.

The dolls soon became enormously popular and adopted as a symbol of "Mother Russia." (Matryoshka means "little mother.") They are turned from a single piece of wood, usually birch or lime, and often painted with scenes from Russian fairy tales, with a different image on each figure.

The inherent charm and intrigue of the nested figures inspired me to use a matryoshka as the magical helper in this original story. While the motifs are Russian, the setting is the universal realm of fairy tales.

It was spring when Katya set out, but the next day there was frost, then snow. It snowed for weeks, as if winter had returned, and Katya was cold and hungry. Often she considered asking the doll for help, but then she would find shelter or a bit of food on her own. Finally she came to a great city. An innkeeper let her stay in the kitchen and fed her bread and soup. "Thank you for your kindness," Katya said. "Please, could you wake me in the morning?"

"Then you will sleep forever, my friend. There is no morning here now," the innkeeper told her. "Ever since the Tsarevitch fell under a wicked spell that turned him into living ice, it is always winter without thaw, night without moon, and dark without dawn."

"A man of ice! What a sight that must be!" said Katya.

"Not a sight for the likes of us," said the innkeeper. "He lies asleep in the palace, watched over by his uncle, the Grand Vizier."

"I have no coin to pay you, but perhaps I can break the spell," Katya said, touching the doll in her pocket. The innkeeper laughed, but Katya was determined to see the man of living ice and to lift the enchantment.

When Katya awoke, it was still dark, but she made her way to the palace, a glorious place of red stone and golden domes. The guards turned her away at the door, but she spied a huge tree in the courtyard. Nimble as a squirrel, Katya climbed its branches and peered through a window. Upon a velvet bed of scarlet and gold lay the Tsarevitch, still and glittering in the candlelight. Behind him stood a tall old man who glared at Katya as he snapped his fingers for his guards. Katya slid down the tree trunk into a circle of grim-faced soldiers.

They took her into the chamber of the frozen prince. Katya had never seen a man so beautiful. His full lips were pale blue and his glassy hands long and fine. His hair glistened like frost. The only sign that he was not a statue carved of ice was the faint cloud of his breath and the slight stirring of his chest. The old man was as red as the prince was blue. His hair and beard glowed like flame and his skin was ruddy.

"Why were you spying on the Tsarevitch?" he demanded.

"Pardon, sir," said Katya. "I only wished to see a man of living ice." Now that she had, she pitied him, trapped in his cold enchantment. She longed to see him awake. "I have come to break the spell."

"You!" scoffed the Grand Vizier. "The wizards of nine kingdoms could not break this spell. Great magic is needed to unweave it, more magic than a peasant girl can imagine." The Grand Vizier had reason to know. He had cast the spell himself to prevent the Tsarevitch from being crowned and to keep the kingdom for his own. It took all of his power to maintain the enchantment.

"But I can break the spell, I swear it!" cried Katya.

"Throw her in the dungeon," ordered the Grand Vizier. The guards took her to a stone prison in a far corner of the palace grounds and down a dark stairway.

The door clanged, shutting Katya inside a tiny cell. She took the nesting doll out of her pocket. "Oh, matryoshka, surely I need help now." Carefully, she twisted off the top half of the smiling doll.

Inside was another figure, not a woman, but a bear. He yawned and stretched, growing until he nearly filled the cell.

The bear said, "So, little one, tell me your need."

"A magic spell has turned the Tsarevitch into living ice and now the kingdom has winter without thaw, night without moon, and dark without dawn," Katya said. "I swore to break the spell. Also, I am not fond of dungeons and would like to get out."

"Dungeon?" said the bear. "Seems a fine cave to me. Still, if you wish to leave, then so we shall. As for the spell, who better than a bear to bring the spring thaw? Climb on my back." Katya put the doll together, slipped it into her pocket, and climbed onto the bear's back. With one huge paw the bear smashed down the door. They rushed up the twisting stair and out behind the palace gardens. The bear gave a great roar and warm wind began to blow. The ice covering the trees began to melt and water dripped from the branches.

"Please, take me to the Tsarevitch," said Katya. She wanted to see him awake. As the bear walked, patches of brown earth filled in his footprints.

The palace guards could not stop the bear, and Katya rode straight to the velvet bed. But the spell was not broken. The prince still slept, though now he looked more ivory than icy blue.

"Something more than my roar is needed," said the bear.

Katya was disappointed, for now she felt more than pity for the enchanted prince, but said, "Thank you, kind bear."

"Keep the doll and remember me," said the bear and vanished.

The Grand Vizier burst into the room with a dozen soldiers, pale with fear and rage. The thaw had weakened his spell—streaks of gray were in his hair and beard. "Seize her!" he shouted.

This time the soldiers took Katya into the forest and tossed her down a deep ravine. Though it was warmer now, the sky was still dark and clotted with clouds. She tried to climb out, but the ravine was too steep and she fell back to the bottom. Katya brushed herself off and took the doll from her pocket.

"Matryoshka, I need your help again," she said, opening the doll. Inside, the bear doll stood still and quiet. She removed it and took off the top half. A wolf twitched an ear, shook his head, and grew until his great gray tail tickled Katya's knees. He turned in a circle, then sat politely before her.

"Small one, tell me your need," he said. Katya told him of the man of ice and the night without moon and dark without dawn and her vow. "Also, I do not wish to sleep in this ravine."

The wolf grinned, saying, "It seems a fine place to rest to me, but leave we shall. As for the other, who better than a wolf to bring back the moon? Come with me." Katya tucked the doll away and climbed onto the wolf's back. The wolf leapt out of the pit and loped through the forest. At the edge of a field he gave a howl that seemed to come from the throats of a thousand wolves. The clouds overhead began to thin, and the face of the moon peered through.

"Please," said Katya. "Take me to the Tsarevitch." As the wolf ran toward the palace, moonlight flowed behind them like a stream.

The guards offered no resistance and they went straight to the Tsarevitch's chamber. He still slept, but now there was a touch of color to his face and hair.

The wolf said, "He needs more than my song to call him back."

Katya sighed, for now she knew she loved the prince, and longed to see him awake for herself, not just because of her vow. She said, "Thank you, kind wolf."

"Keep the doll and remember me," he replied and vanished.

In a corner of the room stood the Grand Vizier. His hair was like frost, his nose like the drip of an icicle. He seemed weak and withered, but his eyes were still fierce as he called for the soldiers to once more take Katya away.

This time the soldiers took her to the top of a mountain. They lowered her by rope onto a ledge and left her there. Katya watched the soldiers ride to the palace through the moonlight.

"I need your help once more, my matryoshka," she said to the doll. Inside the woman was the bear, inside the bear was the wolf. She wondered for a moment what would be next, then twisted the wolf doll apart. Golden light poured out. Nestled in the bottom half was a tiny bird the color of flame. She lifted her head and stretched her wings. In a fiery swirl, she flew up to the top of the mountain and down to Katya's side.

"Tell me your need, my chick," said the firebird.

"Oh, firebird, the Tsarevitch has been turned into ice by a wicked spell. The bear brought back the thaw, the wolf brought back the moon, but still it is dark without dawn across the kingdom," said Katya. "I swore to break this spell, and I do not wish to live on a ledge."

"It seems a fine perch to me, but as you wish. And for the rest, who better than a firebird to bring back the sun?" said she. Katya put the doll together and climbed onto the firebird's back. Up they swooped into the sky, and the firebird burst forth with a great thrill of song. As the last note died away, pink fingers of light stretched over the top of the mountain.

"Please, take me to the Tsarevitch," said Katya. The firebird flew to the palace, sunlight flooding the sky behind them.

They flashed over the heads of the guards and into the Tsarevitch's room.

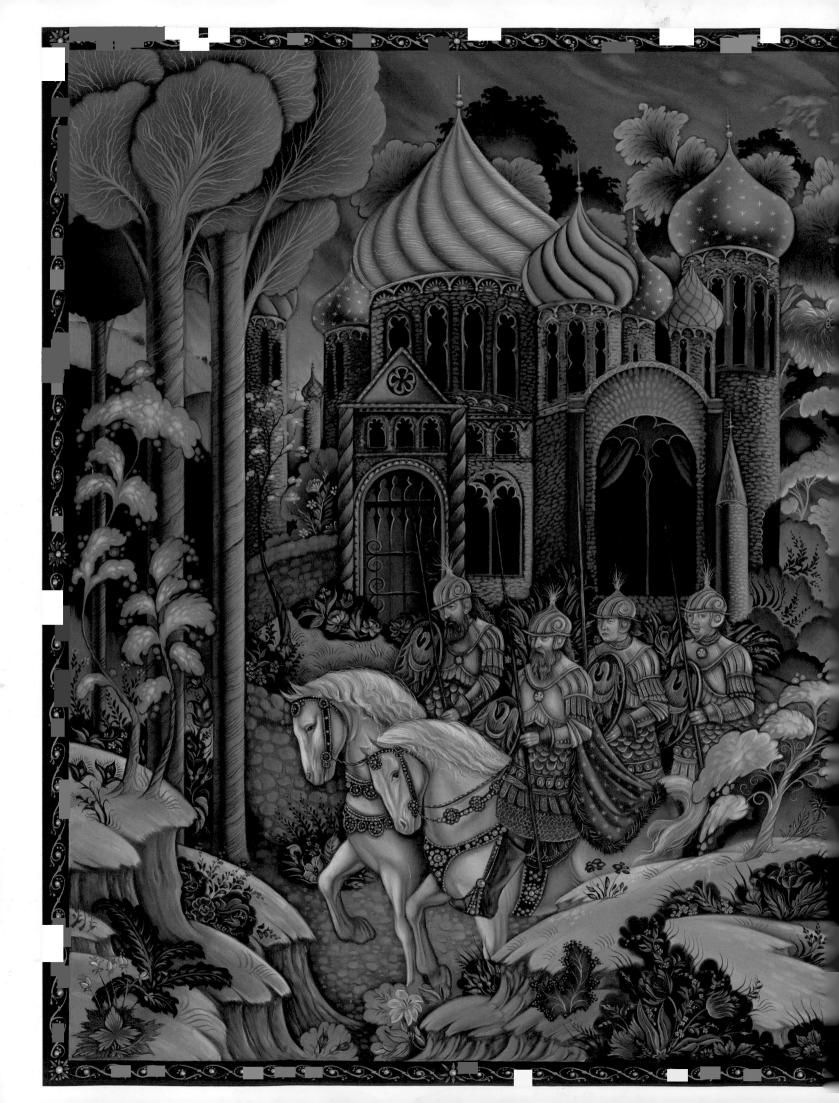

The Grand Vizier stood next to the bed, still as stone. The prince was restored—his hair was brown as earth and his skin warm with life. He stirred as the firebird's light fell across his face, but did not wake.

"Why isn't he awake? Can't you help him?" Katya cried.

"His heart is still frozen. Another kind of magic is needed now," the firebird replied. A strange crackling, snapping sound came from the corner. The Grand Vizier was trying to speak, but his jaw would not move. Now *he* was made of living ice, but his eyes were open, glaring at Katya.

Turning away from the Grand Vizier, Katya said, "Thank you, kind bird. I will find some way to wake the Tsarevitch."

"You have all you need, little pigeon. Keep the doll and remember me," said the firebird, and she vanished.

"I have no more magic to help you," Katya said to the prince. She watched him as she thought. At last she knew what she must do.

"Perhaps the wizards of the nine kingdoms can break the spell now. I will go and find them." She looked down at the prince, more handsome now than ever. Her heart was heavy at the thought of leaving him. Quickly, she bent and kissed him.

Crash! The Grand Vizier toppled over and smashed into a thousand pieces.

"You're real!" said the prince. "I dreamt that a marvelous girl kept coming to me, riding wonderful beasts. And it was you!"

Katya's heart leapt with gladness, for she had found the last bit of magic. As for the prince, what better bride than a girl who could break spells and ride magical beasts? They were married, most happily, of course. As for Katya, what better groom than a man whose heart melts at love's first kiss?

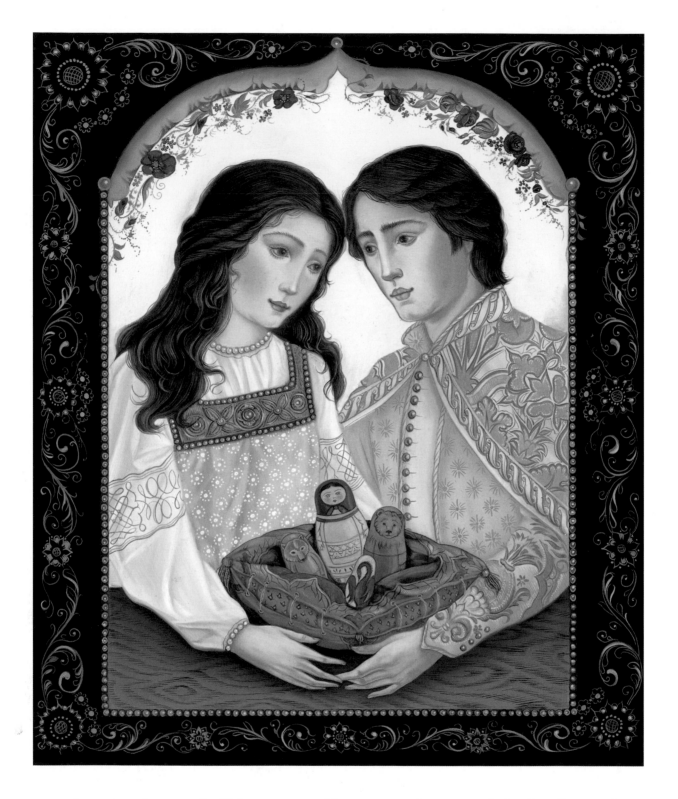

The Tsar banned all hunting of bears, wolves, and firebirds, and
Katya kept the nesting doll in a place of honor
on a cushion from the velvet bed.